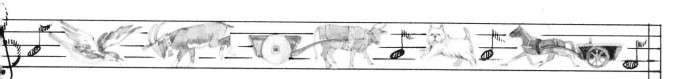

HUSH,
Little Baby

Illustrated by Marlene Ekman

World Book, Inc.
a Scott Fetzer company
Chicago   London   Sydney   Toronto

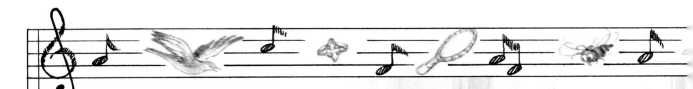

Cover design by Rosa Cabrera
Book design by Ann Tomasic

Hush, little baby,
don't say a word,

Mama's going to buy you
a mockingbird.

If that mockingbird won't sing,

Mama's going to buy you
a diamond ring.

If that diamond ring turns brass,

Mama's going to buy you
a looking glass.

If that looking glass gets broke,

Mama's going to buy you
a billy goat.

If that billy goat won't pull,

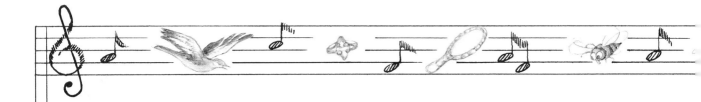

Mama's going to buy you
a cart and bull.

If that cart and bull turn over,

Mama's going to buy you
a dog named Rover.

If that dog named Rover won't bark,

Mama's going to buy you
a horse and cart.

If that horse and cart fall down,

You'll still be the sweetest
little baby in town.

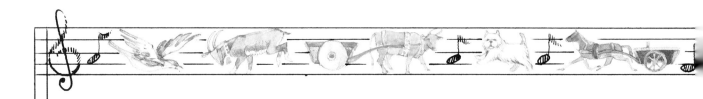

Hush, lit-tle ba - by, don't say a word,

Ma-ma's going to buy you a mock - ing - bird.

If that mockingbird won't sing,
Mama's going to buy you a diamond ring.

If that diamond ring turns brass,
Mama's going to buy you a looking glass.

If that looking glass gets broke,
Mama's going to buy you a billy goat.

If that billy goat won't pull,
Mama's going to buy you a cart and bull.

If that cart and bull turn over,
Mama's going to buy you a dog named Rover.

If that dog named Rover won't bark,
Mama's going to buy you a horse and cart.

If that horse and cart fall down,
You'll still be the sweetest little baby in town.